HOPSCOTCH
ADVENTURES

Sinbad
and the
Pirates

by Martin Waddell and O'Kif

W
FRANKLIN WATTS
LONDON•SYDNEY

First published in 2010 by
Franklin Watts
338 Euston Road
London
NW1 3BH

Franklin Watts Australia
Level 17/207 Kent Street
Sydney
NSW 2000

A CIP catalogue record for this book is available
from the British Library.

ISBN 978 0 7496 9442 5 (hbk)
ISBN 978 0 7496 9448 7 (pbk)

Series Editor: Jackie Hamley
Series Advisor: Catherine Glavina
Series Designer: Peter Scoulding

Printed in China

Franklin Watts is a division of
Hachette Children's Books,
an Hachette UK company
www.hachette.co.uk

One day, Sinbad's ship was captured by pirates.

The pirates made Sinbad's
crew walk the plank.

SPLASH! CRUNCH! SPLASH!
SPLASH! CRUNCH! GURGLE!

"You can be the sharks' first course, Sinbad. I'll be pudding!" groaned Sinbad's friend, Ali. "After you, Ali!" growled Sinbad.

The pirate captain grinned when he heard their names. *"Sinbad the Sailor and Ali?* Someone will pay a king's ransom for you!" he chortled.

"What if no one will pay up?" asked Ali.

"Then snip-snap go the sharks!"
sneered the captain.

"We're doomed!" moaned Ali.

"Maybe," whispered Sinbad. "But we'll sail by the rocks where the sea witches sing. Their song is a powerful spell, and it will send the pirates to sleep. The ship will be wrecked on the rocks."

"Drowned by the sea witches'
spell as we sleep or a snack for
the sharks!" groaned Ali.
"How do we get out of this?"

11

"Think, think, THINK!" Sinbad
said. And he thought...

And he thought...

12

"If we can't hear, we won't fall under the spell!" whispered Sinbad. "Quick, Ali! Call the captain all the rude names you know. Don't argue! Just do it!"

"Stinky Feet! No Brains!" shouted Ali (and lots of other rude names that all sailors know).

"Like what you hear, old Big Ears?" Sinbad asked the pirate captain.

"Big Ears?" roared the angry captain.

"Got you!" thought Sinbad the Sailor.

SLAM-BANG! SLAM-BANG!
"You have a big mouth, but at least I don't have to listen to you now!" sneered the pirate captain.

"What's that? I can't hear a thing with my head stuck in this barrel," mumbled Sinbad.

The ship sailed where the sea
witches sing their strange song.

The witches' beautiful voices soon enchanted the pirates. They fell fast asleep where they stood.

No one steered the ship as it struck
the sea witches' rocks.

Sinbad's ship shattered and sank.

Far away from the power of the
sea witches' spell, Sinbad and
Ali pulled their heads out of
their barrels.

"I couldn't hear anything in there!"
Ali said, rubbing his ears.

"That was the idea," laughed Sinbad the Sailor.

That was the end of the pirates.

Sinbad and Ali were heroes.

Their reward was a chest full
of gold doubloons.

"Home, Big Ears?" smiled Ali.

"I didn't quite 'ear that!" grinned
Sinbad the Sailor.

Puzzle 1

Put these pictures in the correct order.
Which event do you think is most important?
Now try writing the story in your own words!

Puzzle 2

1. Think of something, Sinbad!

2. Everybody walk the plank!

3. Close your ears, Ali!

4. The sea witches are just ahead.

5. Can you hear me, Sinbad?

6. I'll make a fortune from you two.

Choose the correct speech bubbles for the characters above. Can you think of any others? Turn over to find the answers.

Answers

Puzzle 1

The correct order is: 1d, 2f, 3a, 4c, 5e, 6b

Puzzle 2

Sinbad: 3, 4

Ali: 1, 5

The captain: 2, 6

Look out for more Hopscotch Adventures:

TALES OF KING ARTHUR

1. The Sword in the Stone
ISBN 978 0 7496 6694 1

2. Arthur the King
ISBN 978 0 7496 6695 8

3. The Round Table
ISBN 978 0 7496 6697 2

4. Sir Lancelot and the Ice Castle
ISBN 978 0 7496 6698 9

5. Sir Gawain and the Green Knight
ISBN 978 0 7496 8557 7*
ISBN 978 0 7496 8569 0

6. Sir Galahad and the Holy Grail
ISBN 978 0 7496 8558 4*
'SBN 978 0 7496 8570 6

TALES OF ROBIN HOOD

Robin and the Knight
ISBN 978 0 7496 6699 6

Robin and the Monk
ISBN 978 0 7496 6700 9

Robin and the Silver Arrow
ISBN 978 0 7496 6703 0

Robin and the Friar
ISBN 978 0 7496 6702 3

Robin and the Butcher
ISBN 978 0 7496 8555 3*
ISBN 978 0 7496 8568 3

Robin and Maid Marian
ISBN 978 0 7496 8556 0*
ISBN 978 0 7496 8567 6

TALES OF SINBAD THE SAILOR

Sinbad and the Ogre
ISBN 978 0 7496 8559 1*
ISBN 978 0 7496 8571 3

Sinbad and the Whale
ISBN 978 0 7496 8553 9*
ISBN 978 0 7496 8565 2

Sinbad and the Diamond Valley
ISBN 978 0 7496 8554 6*
ISBN 978 0 7496 8566 9

Sinbad and the Monkeys
ISBN 978 0 7496 8560 7*
ISBN 978 0 7496 8572 0

Sinbad and the Giant Spider
ISBN 978 0 7496 9441 8*
ISBN 978 0 7496 9447 0

Sinbad and the Pirates
ISBN 978 0 7496 9442 5*
ISBN 978 0 7496 9448 7

For more *Hopscotch Adventures* and other *Hopscotch* stories, visit:
www.franklinwatts.co.uk

* hardback